MISSING!

D0191278

Flame

Have you seen this kitten?

Flame is a magic kitten of royal blood, missing from his own world.
His uncle, Ebony, is very keen that he is found quickly.
Flame may be hard to spot as he often appears in a
variety of fluffy kitten colours but you can recognize him
by his big emerald eyes and whiskers that crackle with magic!

He is believed to be looking for a young friend to take care of him.

Could it be you?

If you find this very special kitten please let Ebony,
ruler of the Lion Throne, know.

Sue Bentley's books for children often include animals or fairies. She lives in Northampton and enjoys reading, going to the cinema, and sitting watching the frogs and newts in her garden pond. If she hadn't been a writer she would probably have been a skydiver or brain surgeon. The main reason she writes is that she can drink pots and pots of tea while she's typing. She has met and owned many cats and each one has brought a special sort of magic to her life.

Magic Kitten

Seaside Mystery

SUE BENTLEY

Illustrated by Angela Swan

PUFFIN

To Ambrose, teddy-faced ginger tom

PUFFIN BOOKS

Published by the Penguin Group
Penguin Books Ltd, 80 Strand, London WC2R ORL, England
Penguin Group (USA) Inc., 375 Hudson Street, New York, New York 10014, USA
Penguin Group (Canada), 90 Eglinton Avenue East, Suite 700, Toronto, Ontario, Canada M4P 2Y3
(a division of Pearson Penguin Canada Inc.)
Penguin Ireland, 25 St Stephen's Green, Dublin 2, Ireland (a division of Penguin Books Ltd)
Penguin Group (Australia), 250 Camberwell Road, Camberwell, Victoria 3124, Australia
(a division of Pearson Australia Group Pty Ltd)
Penguin Books India Pvt Ltd, 11 Community Centre, Panchsheel Park,
New Delhi – 110 017, India
Penguin Group (NZ), 67 Apollo Drive, Rosedale, North Shore 0632, New Zealand
(a division of Pearson New Zealand Ltd)
Penguin Books (South Africa) (Pty) Ltd, 24 Sturdee Avenue, Rosebank,
Johannesburg 2196, South Africa

Penguin Books Ltd, Registered Offices: 80 Strand, London WC2R ORL, England

puffinbooks.com

Published 2007
4

Text copyright © Sue Bentley, 2007
Illustrations copyright © Angela Swan, 2007
All rights reserved

The moral right of the author and illustrator has been asserted

Set in Bembo
Typeset by Palimpsest Book Production Limited, Grangemouth, Stirlingshire
Made and printed in England by Clays Ltd, St Ives plc

British Library Cataloguing in Publication Data
A CIP catalogue record for this book is available from the British Library

ISBN: 978-0-141-32198-1

Prologue

The young white lion sped across the dusty plain. Flame knew that he must find some cover. It was too dangerous to be out in the open.

Suddenly a terrifying roar rang out and an enormous black adult lion rose from a clump of tall grass and bounded towards him.

'Ebony!'

Flame leapt behind a huge rock. There was a dazzling white flash and where he had once stood now crouched a tiny, long-haired, brown-tabby kitten with a bushy tail.

Flame's heart beat fast in his tiny chest as he backed slowly into a wide crack in the rock. His uncle Ebony was very close. He hoped this disguise would protect him.

The shadow of an enormous paw appeared, centimetres away from the trembling kitten's little brown nose. Flame's emerald eyes sparked with fear and anger as he tensed his muscles ready to fight.

'Stay where you are, Prince Flame. I will protect you,' growled a deep but gentle voice.

Flame sank back in relief as an old grey lion peered in at him. 'I am glad to see you again, Cirrus,' Flame mewed. 'But I do not think even you can protect me from my uncle. He is determined to keep the throne he stole from me, so he can rule in my place!'

Cirrus nodded gravely. 'That is true. It is not safe yet for you to stay here. Use this disguise and go back again to the other world. Hide there until you grow strong and wise and then return to save our land from this evil.'

The tiny kitten looked up into Cirrus's tired old face. 'I will do as you say, old friend. Ebony will not rule forever!'

Cirrus's eyes flickered with affection. He reached a huge paw inside the crack

3

in the rock and gently patted the tiny kitten's head. 'And I cannot wait for that day. Go now, my prince,' he growled softly.

Suddenly another mighty roar rang out. The ground shook as Ebony leapt on to the rock where Flame was hiding.

'Save yourself, Flame! Go quickly!' Cirrus urged.

Sparks glowed in the tiny kitten's long brown-tabby fur. Flame mewed softly as he felt the power building inside him. He felt himself falling. Falling . . .

Chapter
⋆ ONE ⋆

'What a brilliant view!' Maisie Simpson said excitedly. She leaned on her bedroom window sill and peered out of the window.

Sunshine sparkled on the sea, and creamy waves washed on to the nearby sandy beach. Seagulls wheeled above the cliffs, soaring overhead in the clear blue sky.

Maisie and her parents had only just moved to the house in Bridhampton-on-Sea. She was dying to tell her two oldest friends, Jane and Nina, all about it. They had promised to keep in touch, even though Maisie would be living so far away. Maisie had hoped they would phone last night, but neither of them had.

On impulse, she dashed downstairs and phoned each of them in turn. There was no answer from Jane's home phone. Nina was out too. Maisie left her a message on her answerphone.

They've probably gone swimming or are playing tennis, she told herself, trying not to mind that they were having fun without her. It was half-term, after all.

Maisie sighed. She squeezed past the boxes of books and china stacked in the hall and opened the door that led into the old shop on the side of their house.

A loud banging sound met her ears as she went inside. Her dad was painting walls and her mum was up a ladder, putting up shelves. They were both artists and were busy making the old shop into a combined studio and gallery.

Karen Simpson stopped hammering and looked down at her daughter. 'Hello, love. You look a bit glum. Is something wrong?' she asked.

Maisie told her about phoning Jane and Nina. 'They weren't in. And they didn't phone last night. Maybe they've already forgotten all about me.'

'What – in a couple of days? I shouldn't think so,' her mum reasoned. 'I expect they're letting you settle in before they phone. Why don't you try them again later?'

Maisie nodded. 'I will. It's just that . . . I wanted to have a chat with them now.'

Her mum got down the ladder. 'You're really missing your old friends, aren't you?' she said, giving Maisie a hug.

Maisie nodded, feeling a lump rise into her throat.

'It won't be long before term starts, you know. And then you'll make lots of new friends. Am I right or am I right?'

Maisie managed a smile in response. But school didn't start for another two weeks. Right now, it felt more like two years.

James Simpson dropped his wet

paintbrush into the open paint tin. He winked at his daughter. 'I've got a chap coming to set up the computer today. You'll be able to email Jane and Nina to your heart's content tonight.'

'Oh, that's great, Dad!' Maisie felt herself cheering up. She knew that her friends went online for a while most evenings. She would tell them all about her cool new house that had an old sweet shop attached to it!

'In the meantime, if you're bored, you could give me a hand with this painting,' her dad suggested.

Maisie wrinkled her nose. Decorating was definitely not on her list of fun things to do!

'It's a lovely day and the beach looks inviting,' her mum said.

'Or you could . . .' her dad began.

'I think I will go exploring,' Maisie decided hurriedly, before he thought of another job for her to do.

Mrs Simpson chuckled. 'Have a good time and don't go far. Lunch will be ready in an hour or so.'

'OK, Mum! I'll be back by then,' Maisie answered, heading for the door.

She went back through the house and out of the back door. The small back garden was narrow and mostly paved, with plants in big decorative pots. Beyond the garden fence at the bottom, the ground fell away steeply to the beach below.

Maisie opened the gate in the fence and went down the steep flight of stone steps. A warm breeze, smelling of salt, ruffled her shoulder-length brown hair. Once on the beach, she took off her shoes, knotted the laces, and strung them round her neck.

As she padded along, her toes sank into the warm sand. She passed a family with two small children flying a kite. At the edge of the waves, three girls were splashing about and laughing.

Maisie felt a flicker of loneliness. She sighed as she wandered along the beach, stopping now and then to pick up unusual shells. After a few minutes she reached the rocks at the foot of the cliffs.

Shallow pools of water, left behind by the outgoing tide, gleamed in the sun. It was peaceful here with just the sound of the waves and sea birds. The people

on the beach were specks in the
distance.

Maisie found a flattish rock. She sat
down to dangle her bare feet in the
cool water below it as she thought
miserably about how much fun Jane
and Nina would be having back home
without her. Fronds of delicate seaweed
tickled her toes and a prawn scurried

across the sandy bottom. Maisie was leaning forward to look at it when, in the reflection of the water, she suddenly saw a bright silver flash.

'Oh!' She twisted round in surprise. There, standing on a nearby rock, Maisie saw a tiny kitten. It had long brown-tabby fur, a bushy tail, and the brightest emerald eyes she had ever seen. Its fur and whiskers seemed to be glowing with a thousand tiny sparkles of light.

Maisie frowned. Perhaps the kitten was wet for its fur to sparkle like that. The poor little thing did seem to be trembling as if it was cold.

'Hello,' she crooned. 'Where have you come from? What are you doing out here on the rocks, all by yourself?'

The kitten looked up at Maisie with

wide, scared green eyes. 'I come from far away. Can you help me, please?' it mewed.

Chapter
★ TWO ★

Maisie stared at the kitten in utter amazement. She must be even lonelier than she thought. She'd just imagined that the kitten had spoken to her!

Just then a seagull swooped down as if deciding whether the tiny tabby kitten would make a meal. The kitten cringed and yowled with fear.

Maisie jumped up and waved her

arms at the gull to scare it away. 'Leave him alone, you feathered bully!' she cried.

She went towards the kitten and bent down, so that she wouldn't scare it away.

'I wonder what your name is,' she murmured, reaching out to stroke the trembling little body.

The kitten blinked up at her slowly

and some of the fear seemed to fade from its eyes. Despite its tiny size, it didn't seem to be afraid of her.

'I am Prince Flame. What is your name?' it purred.

Maisie jerked her hand back. 'Oh! You really can speak!' she gasped. 'I'm . . . I'm Maisie Simpson. I've just moved into a house near the beach with my parents.' Her curiosity began to get the better of her shock. 'Did you say *Prince* Flame?'

Flame nodded and lifted his tiny head proudly. 'I am heir to the Lion Throne. My uncle Ebony has stolen it and rules in my place. He is fierce and cruel and sends his spies to find me and kill me.'

Maisie shook her head, trying to take it all in. Could everything this tiny cute kitten said be true?

Flame seemed to know what she was thinking. He moved sideways across the rocks away from her.

'Stay back,' he ordered.

There was a blinding silver flash and for a moment Maisie couldn't see anything. But when her sight had cleared, the kitten had gone and in its place a majestic young white lion stood proudly on the rocks.

Maisie gasped, scrambling backwards on her hands and knees. 'Flame?'

'Yes. It is me, Maisie. Do not be afraid,' Flame said in a deep velvety roar.

Before she could say anything, there was another bright flash and instantly Flame was a fluffy, long-haired kitten once more.

'I guess it's all true,' Maisie murmured.

'I need to hide now. Can you help me?' Flame mewed.

Maisie crouched back down again and looked into Flame's big emerald eyes. He was so tiny and helpless-looking. She felt a burst of protectiveness towards him.

'Of course I will. I'll look after you. You can live with me and my parents,' Maisie said, scooping him into her arms.

Flame rubbed his little head against

her arm. 'Thank you, Maisie.'

'I'm going to love having you living with me. Just wait until I tell Mum and Dad about you!'

'No! You must tell no one my secret!' Flame reached up and touched her chin with one tiny, brown-tabby paw. 'Please promise, Maisie.'

Maisie looked down into his serious little face. With his long soft fur, striking tabby markings and bright-green eyes, he was the cutest kitten she had ever seen. She couldn't let him down. 'All right. I promise. I'll just say you're a stray,' she agreed disappointedly.

Flame swished his bushy tail and began purring loudly. 'That is good. Thank you, Maisie.'

★

'Of course you can keep him!' Mrs
Simpson said with a smile, when Maisie
finished explaining where she had
found the tiny kitten. She was in the
kitchen making ham salad sandwiches.
'He's absolutely gorgeous!'

Maisie smiled. She knew her mum
and dad would be fine about Flame
staying.

Mr Simpson patted Flame. 'Fancy a
stray kitten turning up like that, just as

we're moving in. He must be a good-luck token. Maybe you should call him Lucky.'

'But he told me his name . . .' Maisie broke off. She was going to have to be a lot more careful about keeping Flame's secret. 'I um . . . mean, I've already decided to call him Flame,' she said hurriedly.

'Well, I think it suits him,' her mum said. 'I expect Flame's hungry. Kittens need to eat lots of small meals, you know. Why don't you see what you can find for him to eat?'

Maisie cut up a small slice of ham and poured milk for Flame to drink. It wasn't much of a meal, but she'd go to the shops to get some proper cat food later.

Flame chomped the ham and then lapped up the milk, purring loudly.

After lunch, Maisie took Flame upstairs. She laid an old jumper on her duvet and then lifted Flame on to it. He pedalled it into a soft nest with his front paws, and then curled up for a nap.

As Maisie stretched out on the bed beside the sleepy kitten, her face creased in a smile. She still couldn't believe this was happening. A couple of hours ago, she had been feeling lonely and missing her old friends. Now she had made her first new friend. In her wildest dreams, she had never expected him to be a magic kitten!

Chapter
* THREE *

Maisie had been having the most
magical dream. She opened her eyes to
find sunshine pouring through the
bedroom curtains.

Something padded up the duvet with
light steps. Flame sat on her chest and
gave her a whiskery grin. 'Good
morning, Maisie. I slept very well,' he
purred.

Her dream was true! A huge smile spread across Maisie's face as she cuddled Flame and stroked his silky brown-tabby fur.

'Hello, you two! You look nice and cosy!' James Simpson poked his head round Maisie's bedroom door. 'I'm going for an early morning walk along the beach. Do you want to come?'

'Can Flame come too?' Maisie asked.

Her dad grinned. 'Course he can. See you downstairs in two minutes?'

'You're on!' Maisie lifted Flame aside and then threw back the duvet. Leaping out of bed, she pulled on some jeans, a T-shirt and trainers. 'Come on!' she called to Flame, dashing down the stairs with Flame following her.

Her dad was waiting at the back door

with an old canvas bag looped over his
shoulder.

'Is Mum having a lie-in?' Maisie
asked him.

He shook his head. 'She's already in
the old shop, stripping some woodwork.
We'll come back and make her breakfast,
as a surprise.'

'OK,' Maisie agreed.

Flame trotted after Maisie, as she and

her dad went outside and down the
steps to the beach. The tide was out
and the sea was a gleaming silver line in
the distance.

They walked down to where the tide
had washed up bits of seaweed, plastic
bottles, shells and other stuff. Flame
nosed about, crunching up bits of dead
crab and enjoying the interesting smells.

'Yuck! I wouldn't fancy your
breakfast, Flame!' Maisie whispered,
pulling a face.

Flame purred, chewing.

Her dad began sorting through a big
pile of seaweed.

'What are you looking for?' Maisie
asked him.

'I'll give you one guess.'

'Bits of driftwood?' Maisie said.

'Got it in one!' her dad replied.

Maisie grinned at him. Her dad was brilliant at carving birds and small animals. She knew he planned to make some from pieces of sun-bleached drift-wood and sell them in the new gallery.

As Maisie drew closer to the rocks where she had found Flame the previous day, she saw a tall boy poking about in the rock pools. The boy glanced up and saw her. He smiled and waved.

Maisie climbed a steep bank of sand, which had blown against the rocks. Flame scrabbled after her, but his short legs sank into the soft sand. Maisie picked him up and tucked him under one arm.

'Hi. You must be new round here. I'm

Joel Denning,' the boy said with a
friendly smile. He had floppy brown
hair and wore a red T-shirt, cut-off
jeans and battered sandals. He looked
about twelve.

'Hi, I'm Maisie Simpson. I've just
moved here with my parents. That's my
dad back there. We've moved into that
house,' Maisie said, turning and pointing
back up the beach.

'Oh, right. I noticed that someone had moved into the old cottage. Hey, that's a really cute kitten you've got there,' Joel said, noticing Flame peeking out from under Maisie's arm. He reached out to stroke Flame.

Flame purred as Joel rubbed the top of his head.

'Yes. He's called Flame. I . . . haven't had him long,' Maisie told Joel. 'Do you live nearby?'

Joel nodded. 'Just down the road from you.'

James Simpson strolled up to the rocks. He smiled at Joel. 'Hello there. Found anything special?'

'Anemones, limpets, a few crabs,' Joel replied. 'I was hoping I might find a sea cucumber.'

Maisie grinned. 'Yeah, right! Good joke.'

'No, really,' Joel said seriously. 'You can find amazing stuff. I keep a note of everything. See?' He produced a crumpled notebook from his jeans pocket and held it up. 'I write up my notes when I get home.' He flashed Maisie and her dad a grin. 'My dad says I'm keener on animals and plants than I am people!'

Mr Simpson laughed and glanced at Maisie. 'Maybe you'll spend more time outdoors now we live near the sea, instead of playing Eagles and Hawks for hours at a time.'

'Da-ad!' Maisie groaned, going bright red. He could be so embarrassing sometimes.

'What's Eagles and Hawks?' Joel asked, puzzled.

'It's a PlayStation game,' Maisie said, amazed that Joel hadn't heard of it.

'Oh, right. I'm not really into computers.' Joel seemed to lose interest and then his face brightened. 'The best rock pools are at Smuggler's Cove. I'm going there tomorrow. I can show you both if you like.'

'Thanks, but I've a lot of work to do at the house,' Mr Simpson said. 'Why don't you go with Joel, Maisie?'

'I . . . um don't know . . .' Maisie began. She wasn't sure how much fun poking about in pools could be, but maybe it would be better than painting or unpacking, especially if Flame came too. 'All right, I'll come,' she decided.

'Great!' Joel said, beaming. 'I'll call for you in the morning.'

'You will take care, won't you?' Maisie's mum called from the kitchen the following day, as Maisie dashed into the hall.

Joel was waiting at the open front door. 'Don't worry, Mrs Simpson. I know this bit of coast like the back of my hand,' he shouted into the house. He wore walking boots and had a sleeveless jacket with lots of zipped pockets over his shorts.

Without waiting for Maisie to come out of the house, he turned and began sauntering down the road.

Maisie put her shoulder bag on the floor. 'Can you jump inside, Flame? It might be a long walk.'

Flame leapt into the bag with a swish of his tail and Maisie shouldered the bag and hurried after Joel.

'Hey! Wait for us!' she called.

'Us?' Joel turned round with a puzzled look on his face and then noticed Flame's head sticking out of her bag. He frowned. 'What have you brought that kitten for? You'll have to take it back.'

'I'm not leaving Flame behind. Where I go, he goes!' Maisie said firmly.

'Well, OK then,' Joel said grudgingly. 'But make sure you look after him. I don't want him getting in the way when I'm rock-pooling.'

'He won't!' Maisie said. 'Flame's a very unusual kitten. He's ma . . . I mean he understands every word I say.'

'Right.' Joel rolled his eyes before setting off again.

Maisie was starting to think this was a mistake. Joel had seemed friendly the day before, but today he was treating her as if she was a little kid.

She fell into step with him as they turned into a lane and took the cliff path. As they walked along, Joel pointed out tiny islands and told her the names of different rock formations.

Maisie was impressed. She had to admit that Joel knew a lot about this area. She could see that Flame was enjoying himself. He purred as he looked out of her bag at the sea and sniffed the salty air.

After about fifteen minutes, the path sloped downwards until the cliff was more of a steep slope. Joel paused near some large flat rocks and boulders, above a small cove.

Looking down, Maisie saw a semi-circular beach, surrounded by dramatic rocks. 'Wow. Look at that. What an amazing place,' she whispered to Flame.

Flame nodded.

'This is Smuggler's Cove. Wreckers used to lure ships on to those rocks and then steal the cargo,' Joel said, pointing to where the surf was crashing on to some jagged black rocks that stretched out to sea. 'There's a cave a bit further along, where they hid their stuff.'

'Really?' Maisie said, shuddering inwardly. The sunlit cove suddenly seemed sinister and unwelcoming.

Joel glanced at her pale face. 'You

needn't be scared. That was ages ago,' he scoffed.

'I'm not scared,' Maisie said stoutly.

'Good. Because I don't fancy turning back now,' Joel said. 'We can take a short cut down by climbing over these rocks. There's an easier way down, but it's another ten minutes' walk along the cliff path.'

Maisie leaned over a bit. Her tummy clenched as she looked down.

'I'll go first,' Joel said, jumping on to the first rock, and then he glanced back at Maisie. 'On second thought, it's a bit steep if you're not used to it, especially as you're wearing trainers and carrying that kitten. You'd better come down the easier way. Just follow the path. You can't miss the track – it's signposted Smuggler's Cove.'

'But aren't you coming with . . .' Maisie began.

Joel didn't reply. He was already scrambling downwards over the rocks.

Maisie stared down at him. She couldn't believe he had just left her to find her own way down. 'That's just great!' she said to Flame.

Flame pricked up his ears and looked at her enquiringly.

Maisie watched as Joel jumped nimbly down on to the small beach and then turned to look up at her and Flame. 'Are you still there? Hurry up. I'll be just over here!' he called, waving, before turning round and disappearing out of sight behind a big rock.

Maisie clenched her fists. 'Right! I've had about enough of Joel Denning. I'm climbing down there after him. How hard can it be? Hang on, Flame. Here we go.'

Steadying her shoulder bag with one hand, she stepped down on to a large flat rock. Moving slowly and reaching for firm handholds, she climbed down backwards. This was easier than it looked. Now she was almost halfway down.

But on the next rock, her trainer skidded and she slid towards the edge. She grabbed at a nearby rock to steady herself.

'Oh!' Maisie gasped as the rock moved under her hand and she lost her balance. She scrabbled for a foothold, but her foot slipped again and she found herself kicking out at thin air.

Chapter
★ FOUR ★

Time seemed to stand still. Flame
sprang out of the shoulder bag and
landed on the rock above Maisie.

His long, brown-tabby fur glittered
with sparks and his whiskers crackled
with electricity. A warm tingling feeling
flowed down Maisie's spine.

Flame raised a tiny paw and a fountain
of bright silver sparks shot towards

Maisie. They swirled round her like a snowstorm.

'Oo-oh!' Maisie cried as her whole body slid backwards. She screwed her eyes shut and prepared herself for a very painful landing.

But she didn't fall. Instead, Maisie felt herself sinking down slowly and gently. Her eyes shot open and she realized

that she was encased in a big sparkling bubble. The bubble, with Maisie inside, landed on the beach. It bobbed up and down gently before settling and then disappeared with a faint pop!

Flame sprang down and landed beside Maisie. Every last trace of sparks had faded from his fur.

Maisie's knees suddenly gave way and she sat on the sand. Although she was safe now, she still felt shaken up.

Flame jumped into her lap. 'Are you hurt?' he mewed anxiously.

'No. But only thanks to you. You were brilliant, Flame! I didn't know you could do that! Thanks for saving me,' she said, kissing the top of his silky little head.

'You are welcome,' Flame purred.

Joel appeared from behind the rock.
His eyebrows lifted in surprise when he
saw Maisie sitting on the sand. He
marched towards her, a fierce frown on
his face.

'You've gone and hurt yourself,
haven't you? I told you not to climb
down!' he shouted.

Maisie felt her cheeks reddening with
anger. 'You just left me up there by
myself!' she shouted back.

'Because I thought you might fall,
you stupid kid!' Joel snapped.

Maisie lost her temper. She jumped to
her feet and put her hands on her hips.
'You're just a fat-headed idiot, who likes
ordering people about! I wish I hadn't
bothered to come. I'm going home,
right now!' she yelled.

Joel's mouth dropped open as Maisie turned on her heel. 'Go on then! See if I care,' he called after her.

Tears of anger pricked Maisie's eyes as she found the track and stormed up the shallow rocky slope to the cliff path.

Flame scampered over the rocks and gullies, trying to keep up. He gave a frustrated little miaow as he struggled to climb out of a gap between two rocks.

Maisie slowed down and lifted him into her shoulder bag. 'Sorry, Flame,' she apologized. 'I didn't mean to march off like that.'

She put her hand inside her bag and stroked his long soft fur as she walked along. Thank goodness she had Flame

for her friend because it didn't look like
she had any others now.

Maisie had just about calmed down
by the time she and Flame reached
home.

She sneaked quietly into the house,
hoping to avoid awkward questions
about why she was back so early.

Luckily her parents were still working in the old shop.

Her heart lifted when she saw the computer was set up on a wooden desk in the corner of the sitting room. She went to switch it on, but nothing happened.

'Oh, great,' she murmured. 'I still can't find out if Jane and Nina want to be my friends.' It felt so weird not to be in touch.

Her dad came into the room and saw her standing by the computer. 'Hello, love. I'm afraid it's not working yet. The computer man can't come to sort the internet out for a few more days. How was Smuggler's Cove?'

'OK. But a bit creepy too,' she replied. 'Joel said that wreckers lured ships on to the rocks, so they could rob them.'

'Where's Joel? Did he come back with you?'

'No. I don't know where he is,' Maisie said vaguely. 'What's for lunch?' she asked, changing the subject.

Her dad gave her a searching look, but didn't say anything.

'I wonder who that can be,' Maisie said to Flame later that afternoon as she went to answer the front door.

Joel stood there with his hands behind his back and a sheepish look on his face. There was a girl with him. She was small with short brown hair and a pretty, round face and looked about eleven years old.

Maisie blinked at them in surprise. She hadn't expected to see Joel again so soon. 'What do you want?' she said stiffly.

'Er . . . hi,' Joel said awkwardly. 'This . . . um, is my sister Louise.'

Louise smiled at Maisie, her brown eyes sparkling. 'Hi. Joel told me that you two had an argument this morning. He can't help being an idiot sometimes. It's because he's wildlife mad. He thinks everyone should take it as seriously as he does.' She grinned and nudged her brother. 'Give them to her then, you wally!'

'All right, I was just going to!' Joel blushed and held out a pair of battered walking boots. 'These don't fit me any more. I thought you might be able to use them for climbing rocks and stuff. They're better than trainers. And . . . um, sorry about shouting at you earlier,' he mumbled.

Despite herself, Maisie smiled. 'That's OK,' she said as she reached for the boots. 'I'm sorry too. I shouldn't have lost my temper. Thanks for the boots.'

'Thank goodness for that!' Louise gave her brother a friendly shove and then turned back to Maisie. 'Now we can all be friends. You and I are going to be in the same year at school when term starts, you know.'

'Are we? Right . . .' Maisie said, liking Joel's forceful sister more every minute. School was certainly going to be interesting with her around.

Louise looked down to where Flame

was standing by Maisie's ankle. Her eyes lit up. 'Oo-ooh! What a gorgeous kitten. Can I pick him up?'

Maisie nodded. 'But be careful. He's only tiny.'

'I will. Don't worry.' Louise bent down and scooped Flame up. She held him close to her chest and scratched

him very gently under his chin. 'Hello, you,' she crooned.

Flame purred loudly and closed his eyes with pleasure.

Seeing that Flame felt secure, Maisie relaxed. She suddenly remembered her manners and opened the front door wide. 'Why don't you both come in? I'll show you around and you can meet my mum and dad.'

Louise stepped inside, still carrying Flame. 'I thought you'd never ask!'

Maisie took Joel and Louise through to the old shop where her parents were working, and introduced them. 'Look what I've got. Joel gave me them,' she said, holding up the boots.

'That was kind of you, Joel,' Mrs Simpson said, wiping her hands on a cloth. Joel blushed. He looked at the half-painted walls, wooden shelving and bare floorboards. 'It looks really different in here. Lighter and sort of . . . bigger.'

'Duh! That's because there's no brown wallpaper or counter with musty newspapers, and no shelves with jars of sticky old sweets,' Louise said.

'Is that how it used to be? The old shop sounds like a nightmare,' said Mr Simpson.

Joel and Louise laughed.

Maisie smiled at her parents. They were brilliant at making people feel at ease. She showed her new friends the rest of the house and then brought them back to the kitchen. They sat at the table. 'Would you two like to stay for supper?' she asked Joel and Louise.

Louise answered. 'Thanks, but we'd better get back. Mum will be expecting us. Come on, Joel.'

Maisie picked up Flame, who was curled up on her lap, and went to the door. 'Bye. See you!' she called as Joel and Louise left.

'We're going on a bike ride to Smuggler's Cove tomorrow and taking a picnic with us. Do you want to come?' Louise said.

'You can wear your new boots,' Joel encouraged.

As Flame gave an extra-loud purr, Maisie grinned. 'We'd love to!'

Chapter
★ FIVE ★

Maisie's hair streamed out behind her
as she cycled along the following
morning.

Flame was in the basket attached to
the handlebars. He leaned forward, his
nose twitching as he snuffled up the
exciting smells.

Maisie could see Joel and Louise up
ahead. They were having a race to see

who could reach the top of the hill
first.

'I won!' shouted Joel, waving both
arms in the air.

'Only because you've got longer legs
than me!' Louise cried. She turned
round and cycled back towards Maisie.
'Almost there now. Smuggler's Cove is
just round the headland.'

'Great,' Maisie said, pedalling hard as

Louise wheeled around again and sped after her brother once more. 'Phew! Those two are some double act! I can hardly keep up with them!' she said to Flame.

Flame nodded, his bright emerald eyes sparkling. 'Are we a double act too?'

'We're the best ever!' Maisie said, feeling her heart swell with affection for the tiny kitten.

Smuggler's Cove had a picnic area on the cliff top. There was a small car park and a kiosk selling ice cream and drinks. Maisie lifted Flame out of the basket and then chained her bike up. Joel and Louise chained their bikes next to hers.

They sat on the grass to eat. The food was delicious and Maisie ate hungrily.

She broke bits off her cheese sandwich for Flame.

Joel was wearing his sleeveless jacket with all the pockets. He sprawled on his stomach to eat his crisps. He'd almost finished them when Louise jumped on him. The crisps shot everywhere.

'Hey! I hadn't finished those!' Joel complained crossly.

'Tough! You have now!' Louise said, giggling as she wrestled with her brother and tried to stuff grass into his mouth.

Maisie laughed. They were completely mad. She hoped that they didn't decide to start on her!

After a few minutes, Joel and Louise sat up. Joel's jacket and Louise's T-shirt were covered in grass stains.

'Let's go and explore the caves,' Joel suggested, shaking his head to get grass out of his hair.

'Do you think we should? Maisie might be scared,' Louise panted, her brown eyes gleaming mischievously.

'Scared? Why would I be?' Maisie asked.

'Because of the legend,' Louise said,

winking at her brother. 'A smuggler was trapped inside the cave by the rising tide. Sea monsters swam up and dragged him away. Sometimes you can still hear his screams.'

'I really believe that!' Maisie scoffed, laughing.

But even though she knew Louise was just teasing, she had a horrid squirmy feeling in her tummy. In her imagination, she could hear the blood-curdling screams echoing round the lonely caves.

'Shut up, Lou, you're scaring her,' Joel said. He got up and started walking down the grassy slope.

'Aw, she's not scared! Are you?' Louise said, beckoning to Maisie and Flame. 'Come on, let's go!'

Flame trotted along at Maisie's heels
as she made her way down to the small,
sheltered cove. They had to scramble
over seaweed-draped rocks at the mouth
of the cave.

Maisie frowned as she entered the
shadowy cave. It was very dark at the
back, where the sunlight didn't reach.
Rocks were spread over the cave's sandy
floor. Small pools of cold dark water
were dotted among them.

'Come on, you lot!' Joel called
hollowly from deep inside.

'We're coming! Hold your horses!'
Louise shouted, disappearing into the
shadows.

Maisie told herself there was nothing
to be scared of as she went further into
the cave after Louise and Joel. 'Are you

all right, Flame? Do you want me to pick you up?' she whispered.

'I am fine, thank you, Maisie,' Flame answered, placing each tiny brown-tabby paw with deliberate care as he followed her over the rocks. Silver sparks shone faintly in his long silky fur.

Maisie shivered. It was getting chilly
and smelt of damp and old seaweed.
Every slight sound seemed magnified
and spooky. There was no sign of Joel
or Louise. She was really glad she had
Flame with her.

Maisie was thinking of turning back,
and risking being teased for being
chicken, when she noticed the natural
shelves in the cave walls. There was
lots of driftwood there, washed up
by the high tide when it filled the
cave.

'Wow! Look at all that brilliant wood.
Dad would love it for his carvings,' she
said to Flame.

'Perhaps you should tell him it is here
and then he can come and get it,'
Flame purred.

'Better than that, I'll take some back for him as a surprise!' Maisie said.

She clambered towards the side of the cave and began collecting driftwood. Flame watched her from where he sat on a rock beside a large pool behind her.

'Who-oo-oooh!' Suddenly a terrible wail rang out, echoing round the cave creepily.

'Oh!' Maisie gasped, as her heart missed a beat. It was the drowned smuggler!

Then things seemed to happen all at once. Maisie heard Joel and Louise scream with fear and then their foot-steps rang on the rocks as they pounded towards her.

Just as Joel and Louise came into sight, Flame screeched with panic.

Maisie turned to see him scrabbling for a paw-hold on the seaweed. As she watched, he fell with a sickening splash into the pool.

Chapter
* SIX *

'Flame!' Maisie cried in horror.
Dropping the driftwood, she sprang
towards the rocks.

'What's happened? Where is he?' Joel
shouted, rushing up with Louise close
behind him.

'He's under the water!' Maisie pointed
at the pool, her heart pounding.

Flame's tiny head suddenly appeared.

He paddled desperately, his paws
sending out ripples as he trod water.

'Swim to the side, Flame! You should
be able to climb out,' Maisie urged,
hoping that the other two wouldn't
realize that Flame actually understood.

Flame mewed and swam towards the
side of the pool, where thick seaweed
from the rocks draped into the water.
He tried to catch hold with his claws,
but it was no use and he slipped back in.

'He can't get out. He'll be drowned!'
cried Louise.

Maisie felt desperate. She realized that Flame couldn't use his magic without giving himself away. Before she could think twice about it, she stepped forward and launched herself into the pool.

She gasped with shock as the icy water rose almost up to the tops of her thighs and a dreadful pain shot up her leg. She had twisted her ankle on a submerged rock.

A wave of sickness washed over Maisie, but she gritted her teeth. Flame had sunk for a second time. She plunged her hands beneath the water and felt around.

'Got you!' she cried as her fingers closed over wet fur.

She lifted Flame up triumphantly and

held him to her chest. Shivering and whimpering with cold, Flame clung to her soaked T-shirt.

Joel and Louise leaned over to help Maisie clamber out of the pool. Trying not to put any weight on her twisted ankle, she crawled on to the rocks on her hands and knees.

Still holding Flame, Maisie managed to sit up. Her ankle throbbed with a dull ache and she was shivering from head to foot. She bit her lip as a small groan escaped her.

'What's wrong? Are you hurt, Maisie?' Louise asked with concern.

'She's probably just cold. What did you jump in for, you idiot?' Joel scolded Maisie, white-faced.

'Shut up, Joel! And give her your

jacket,' Louise ordered, glaring at him.

Joel quickly took off his jacket and
spread it round Maisie's shoulders. As
soon as Flame was covered up, Maisie
felt sparks igniting in his fur and gently
prickling her fingers.

A familiar warm tingling flowed down her spine. She felt deep, soothing heat spreading all over her body until her shivering gradually stopped. She gasped as the pain in her ankle increased for a second and then it seemed to pour away, like water down a drain.

Flame snuggled up to her, his tiny body warm once more and his silky fur as soft as thistledown. As every last spark faded, his whole body vibrated with his purring.

'Stay with Maisie, Louise, I'll run and get help!' Joel cried.

Maisie realized that what had felt like minutes passing, while Flame performed his magic, had actually only been seconds. 'No! Wait!' she called after Joel. 'I'm feeling much better now. And Flame's OK too. Let's just keep this between ourselves. If my parents hear about this, I'll be grounded until term starts!'

'You've got a point,' Joel agreed. 'Our mum and dad won't be too thrilled either. I'm the oldest, so I'll get the blame for bringing you here.'

'But are you sure you're all right?'
Louise looked closely at Maisie and
Flame. 'I don't get it. You're hardly
even wet. It's like magic,' she said in
amazement.

Maisie smiled to herself, wishing she
could tell them how wonderful Flame
really was. She sighed as she thought about
how she could never tell anyone. 'I'm fine,'
she said firmly. 'Come on. Let's go!'

'I've just thought what might make that
awful shrieking sound,' Joel said, as they
retraced their steps back to Smuggler's
Cove. 'The wind blowing through a
hole in the top of the cave.'

'Now he tells us!' Louise said, rolling
her eyes and giving her brother a
punch on the arm.

'Ow!' Joel rubbed his arm and took a pretend swing at his sister.

Maisie bit back a grin as Joel and Louise squabbled. At least things were back to normal.

As she lifted Flame into her bike's basket, she bent over and whispered, 'Are you OK now?'

Flame licked her chin with the tip of his rough little tongue. 'I am fine. Thank you for saving me, Maisie. You were very brave,' he purred.

'I wasn't really. I just couldn't bear to think of anything happening to you,' she whispered fondly.

She realized that it was true. She couldn't imagine not having Flame around. Maisie felt a pang at the thought that one day he would have to go back to his home world. She shuddered and decided that she wasn't going to think about that.

Chapter
★ SEVEN ★

A couple of days later, Maisie was
helping her mum put books on to
shelves and stack china in cupboards.

Flame was curled up on the sunny
sitting-room window sill, dozing.

'A week's gone by already,' Mrs
Simpson said. 'It's only a few days
before we open the new gallery.'

'I know. Everything seems to be

happening at once!' Maisie said. The computer was also finally set up and working.

Maisie had discovered that Jane and Nina had sent her long emails, and had both been worried when Maisie hadn't replied for a few days. Now she was in touch with her friends and they were sharing news and chatting just like always.

Maisie had been emailing last night and received some brilliant news. Both of them, with their families, were coming down for the grand opening at the weekend. 'I can't wait to show Jane and Nina Smuggler's Cove and introduce them to Joel and Louise.'

Mrs Simpson smiled, but she looked

a bit worried. 'It'll be lovely for you
to have your old friends here. But
I hope we'll have the gallery ready
in time. There seems so much to
do.'

Maisie went over and gave her mum
a hug. 'Don't worry. Flame and I will
help you. Won't we, Flame?'

Flame blinked at her with bright-
green eyes.

'You and your imagination, Maisie
Simpson,' her mum exclaimed. 'You talk
as if that kitten's capable of anything!
Maybe I should give him a mop and a
bucket!'

Maisie smiled inwardly, as a cute
picture of Flame cleaning the floor with
a tiny mop came into her mind. *If only
you knew*, she thought.

★

Maisie and Flame were in the old shop by themselves the next day, helping to decorate it. Mrs Simpson had gone into town to buy food and Mr Simpson had gone in search of a furniture shop.

'Yeah! Go for it!' Maisie clapped her hands as the brush rose into the air and then dipped itself into the pot of varnish with a flourish. It wiped itself carefully on the rim before dancing across the wooden counter, a comet's trail of silver sparks shooting out behind it.

'Must work hard, must work hard!' the brush sang softly to itself.

'Decorating's much more fun with you helping, Flame!' Maisie said, giggling.

Flame sat on the floor, grooming his twinkling brown-tabby fur. He looked up from nibbling his front paw and grinned at Maisie. 'I am glad I can be of help!'

Maisie heard the sound of footsteps. 'Quick! Someone's coming!'

A spark shot out of Flame's paw and the brush fell silent. It zoomed back to the open varnish tin and laid itself across the top. Every last gleaming silver spark disappeared from Flame's fur.

Maisie rushed over and picked up the brush, just as her dad came into the shop carrying a flat cardboard box under one arm.

He blinked with surprise when he saw the brush in Maisie's hand. 'Goodness me, you've been busy! You're doing a grand job on that counter,' he said.

Maisie blew on her nails and polished them on her T-shirt. 'Does that mean I can have an increase in my pocket money?' she asked, grinning.

Her dad chuckled. 'Nice try! I'll think about it! Especially if you help me assemble this cabinet. It's one of those make-it-yourself items.'

Maisie groaned inwardly. The words 'make-it-yourself' and 'dad' put together, could mean trouble.

If only she could think of a way of getting her dad to go out again for a little while. Flame would have the cabinet assembled in a few sparkly seconds. But Mr Simpson was already rolling up his sleeves, a determined look on his face.

'Right! Where's the instructions?' he murmured, tearing open the box.

Maisie's heart sank as she knelt on the floor and started to help her dad.

An hour and a half later, sections of the unmade cabinet and little plastic packets of screws and bolts were strewn all around.

Flame sniffed at one of the bags and batted it with one paw.

Maisie quickly rescued the screws as they skidded across the room. 'No, Flame. Leave those alone, please,' she scolded gently. She looked at her dad. 'Maybe you should get Mum to help you when she gets back from the shops,' she suggested.

'I think you're right,' her dad said, exasperated. He stood up with a heavy sigh and mopped his forehead on his shirtsleeve. 'I give up! Who writes these instructions anyway? They should be locked up!'

'Never mind, Dad,' Maisie said, trying hard not to laugh. 'It did look really complicated. I think Flame and I will go to the beach if you don't need us any more.'

'Good idea. Are you going to call for Joel and Louise?' he asked.

Maisie shook her head. 'They had to go shopping for school uniforms with their mum. Anyway, I've got Flame for company. He's the best friend anyone could have.'

Mr Simpson smiled and reached

down to pat Flame. 'Have a good time, you two. And don't forget to keep your eyes open for any interesting bits of driftwood.'

'Definitely,' Maisie said. 'Come on, Flame.'

Flame scampered after her as she went into the house and out to the front garden. Her bike was leaning against the house wall. She wheeled it out on to the street.

Flame's forehead wrinkled in a frown. 'I do not think we need the bike to go to the beach, Maisie.'

'No. But we do if we're going to Smuggler's Cove,' Maisie said. 'Remember all that fantastic driftwood we saw in the cave? They were huge bits. I'm going to get some for Dad. I reckon he needs cheering up after that defeat with the display cabinet.'

Flame nodded. 'That is a kind thought. Perhaps you should tell him where you are going or ask him to come too?'

Maisie thought about it. She had a niggling feeling that if she mentioned Smuggler's Cove her dad would say it was too far to go by herself. But if she didn't ask him, he couldn't tell her not to go.

'We're all ready now. Let's just go,' she decided. 'We won't be long.'

Flame mewed an agreement as she lifted him into the bike's front basket and they set off.

Rain clouds were gathering overhead and there was a cool breeze, but Maisie hardly noticed the weather as she cycled along the cliff path. It was perfect, just being with Flame. He sat up in front of her, his ears pricked and his little front paws resting over the rim of the basket.

The small car park at Smuggler's Cove was almost empty. There were no picnickers today, only a couple of people sitting on a bench looking out to sea. The girl in the ice-cream kiosk was reading a book.

Maisie chained up her bike and set off down the grassy slope to the cove with Flame at her heels. They soon came to the mouth of the cave and carefully climbed over the rocks to get inside.

Maisie couldn't suppress a shudder as

she stood on the cave's sandy floor.
There was a slimy green mark about a
metre high up the rocky sides, where
the water obviously come up to when
the tide came in.

When they had last come here it had
been a bright sunny day, but the cave
had seemed damp and spooky. Today, it
seemed even more shadowy and

gloomy. Maisie bit her lip, recalling Louise's scary tales of trapped smugglers being dragged away by sea monsters.

'Is something wrong?' Flame mewed.

'Not really. It's just this place. It gives me the creeps,' Maisie replied. 'Let's get some driftwood and go.'

Flame nodded. Suddenly he sat up straight and peered intently into the cave, as if he could hear something.

'What is it . . .?' Maisie began and then she froze.

Muffled sounds reached her. A burst of hollow laughter swelled in the air, echoing off the cave walls at the back. It gradually got louder as if someone, or something, was coming closer.

Maisie's eyes widened as a strange figure loomed out of the shadows. It

seemed to have a round back and lots
of dark shiny legs. Her blood ran
cold as the weird creature crawled over
the rocks towards her.

Chapter
★ EIGHT ★

'Argh! M . . . Monster! Flame . . . help
. . .' Maisie stammered.

She couldn't move. The stories were
true. Sea monsters really did live in the
cave!

Beside her, Flame hissed. Maisie saw
sparks in his fur and then was surprised
as they quickly went out as the figure
came closer into the light.

Maisie dared to look back at the cave.

Relief washed over her. It was six teenage kids in wetsuits, holding their dinghy above their heads. There wasn't any monster after all.

Maisie gave a shaky laugh as the teenagers ran past her and headed for the cave's entrance. 'Hi!' they called, waving and laughing.

'Hi!' Maisie waved back.

She watched them put the dinghy down into the shallow water washing around the cave's entrance. Some of the teenagers jumped in and the others dragged the dinghy out of sight. Just as they disappeared from view, one of them shouted to Maisie.

'Don't hang about in here. Watch out for the . . .' Whatever else he said was lost in the sound of the waves crashing on the rocks in the distance.

As soon as they were alone, Maisie turned to Flame. 'Phew! I was really scared for a minute! Mum always says my imagination works overtime!'

Flame gave her a whiskery grin and rubbed himself against her ankles. 'I thought it was a sea monster too!'

Maisie bent down and patted him

affectionately. 'Did you? I don't feel such a wimp then! Come on. Let's get some driftwood!'

She climbed up to the natural rocky shelves and began collecting big pieces of the twisted, bleached wood. Her dad could make some fantastic carved birds from this. When she had enough to almost fill the bike's basket, she clambered back down on to the cave's sandy floor.

'Oh!' she gasped, looking down in dismay as cold seawater swirled round her ankles.

She looked back towards the cave's entrance and saw that the sea was washing up the sides of the rocks there. The tide was coming in fast. With a gulp, Maisie now realized what the teenager had been trying to warn her about.

She suddenly remembered the high tidemark on the cave walls. How long would it be before the cave was flooded?

'We're trapped, Flame! We're going to have to swim for it!' she cried.

Maisie stared in horror at the entrance to the cave. The cold grey sea was flowing in ever faster. The thought of having to swim round the cove and back to the beach terrified her.

Sparks ignited in Flame's long brown-tabby fur and his whiskers crackled with electricity. Maisie felt a familiar warm prickling sensation down her spine.

'Follow me!' Flame's eyes glowed like green coals. With a shower of bright sparks, he leapt from rock to rock, speeding towards the cave's entrance and the rising water.

'Wait!' Maisie pleaded, hesitating. 'I can't, Flame. I'm too scared!'

'Trust me!' Flame called and then he leapt into the cold swirling water.

Maisie felt her whole body fill with a strange tingling. Her feet moved all by themselves and she found herself running after him. A flash of energy shot up her spine. She rushed forward to the mouth of the cave and her muscles tensed as she sprang up into a mighty leap.

In a flash, she dived straight into the sea. With a flick of her powerful tail and flippers, she cut through the water. Her body had become strong and streamlined and covered with smooth grey skin.

Flame had turned her into a dolphin!

There was a rush of water against Maisie's elongated face and she shot through the waves in a stream of bubbles. Shoals of silver fish darted aside as she dived down. She used her flippers and tail to steer herself back around to the cove, avoiding the sharp rocks.

Leaping out of the water with sheer excitement, Maisie performed a set of somersaults, and then it was time to swim towards the shore.

Maisie felt herself carried on the crest of a wave. She coasted along at high speed, like an expert surfer, riding the waves rolling towards the shore.

As Maisie's feet touched the sandy bottom, she stood up. Feet! She was a girl again. Maisie ran up the beach, surprised to find that she was completely dry.

Flame came bounding down the sand towards her.

'Wow! Thanks, Flame. That was brilliant. I loved being a dolphin!' she said, her chest swelling with relief and happiness. 'And I love having you for a friend. I hope you stay with me forever!'

Flame's emerald eyes twinkled with affection. 'I will stay as long as I can,' he answered in a soft purr that held a note of sadness.

Chapter
★ NINE ★

'Oh, well. Dad's still going to have to
go without his driftwood . . .' Maisie
commented, as she and Flame trudged
up the beach and began the walk back
towards Smuggler's Cove.

Flame's eyes twinkled, but he didn't
reply.

Maisie's legs were aching by the time
she and Flame had climbed the long

slope up to the car park. But as she walked towards her bicycle, her face lit up. The basket was filled to bursting with some of the best pieces of drift-wood!

'Oh, Flame, you're wonderful! You think of everything,' she said.

Flame gave a modest purr. 'I try to!'

Maisie lifted him on to the stacked

wood, before unchaining her bike and cycling home. She smiled to herself as she rode along, remembering the fantastic feeling of being a dolphin and swimming under the sea.

She knew she'd never forget the experience.

A few spots of rain began to fall as she cycled up to Joel and Louise's house.

Their car was parked outside. Joel and Louise were just getting out. Both of them held plastic carrier bags. Maisie braked and stopped.

'Hi! Have you and Flame been anywhere interesting?' Joel asked.

'Nah! Just collecting stuff for my dad!' Maisie said vaguely. Joel wouldn't believe her if she told him the truth,

even if she had been able to! 'How
about you two? Did you have a good
time in town?'

'Duh! What do *you* think? We were
shopping for school kit,' Louise said,
pulling a face.

Maisie laughed. In all the excitement
she had forgotten what Joel and Louise
had been doing. 'Oh, yeah! Poor you.

Do you fancy meeting up later?'

Joel looked up at the sky, where thick grey clouds were gathering. 'There's not much point. It's going to chuck it down. We can't go to the beach or go birdwatching or anything.'

'But we could go to Maisie's house and play Eagles and Hawks,' Louise suggested.

Maisie's head came up. 'I never knew you liked playing computer games!'

'You never asked me. I love them. It's Joel who isn't bothered. He'd rather scribble in his old notebook about boring plants and creepy old insects.'

Joel scowled at his sister. 'Hey! Wildlife isn't boring!'

'Course it's not,' Maisie said quickly, seeing another squabble brewing. 'I like

wildlife-watching *and* computers.
Anyway, I've got to go home now. Why
don't you both come round later?'

'OK. See you!' Joel and Louise
chorused as Maisie rode away.

'Those two!' Maisie said to Flame,
with a grin. 'I reckon they'd argue that
cornflakes were custard!'

A crack of thunder rumbled overhead.
Lightning flashed across the sky outside
Maisie's bedroom window as she
entered her room.

'Flame? Where are you?' she said,
peering around.

Strange. Flame usually followed her
everywhere, but he had disappeared the
minute lunch was over. She had
searched for him downstairs, but he was

nowhere in sight. Maybe he had come up here for a nap.

'Joel and Louise have just arrived. Aren't you coming downstairs to watch us play?' she said encouragingly.

Suddenly she noticed a small lump under her duvet. As she lifted it up, she saw Flame's bushy tail sticking out from under a pillow.

'What's this – hide and seek?' she

asked, smiling. But Maisie's face fell as Flame turned and looked at her with dull emerald eyes.

An awful suspicion was dawning on her. 'It's your uncle's spies, isn't it? Have they come for you?'

Flame nodded, trembling all over. 'I can sense them. They are nearby. But they may pass by if I stay very quiet and still,' he mewed softly.

'But . . . what if they don't go past?' she gulped.

'I will have to leave, quickly, to save myself,' Flame mewed.

'I understand,' Maisie said in a small voice, her chest tightening with fear for him. It was horrible to think of Flame leaving, but far worse to think of him being hurt. She made herself answer calmly. 'I'm staying here with you. I'll go and tell Joel and Louise I've changed my mind about playing games.'

Flame shook his head and curled himself into an even tighter ball. 'No, Maisie. You will only draw attention to me. Leave me here, please.'

'All right.' Maisie tucked the duvet up high around the pillows. No one would know that a tiny kitten was hiding there. 'I . . . I'll see you later,' she said, going out on to the landing.

At least, I hope I will, she thought, as she went slowly downstairs.

There was an ache in her throat as she bit back tears. She could hardly believe that Flame might have to leave so suddenly and without even saying goodbye.

Chapter
★ TEN ★

Maisie waved goodbye to Joel and Louise at the front door. 'See you tomorrow for the gallery's grand opening!'

'You bet!' Louise said, grinning.

'Thanks for the game. Are you . . . um, sure you're OK?' Joel asked, looking concerned.

'I promise,' Maisie said, smiling. She

felt bad that she'd been a bit quiet during the game, but she couldn't stop worrying about whether Flame would still be there.

The second they had gone, Maisie whipped round and hurtled up the

stairs two at a time. She slowly pushed open her bedroom door, her heart in her mouth.

'Flame!' she exclaimed.

He sat on the bed cleaning his whiskers. As soon as he saw Maisie, he mewed a greeting. Jumping off the bed, Flame ran towards her, his bushy tail sticking up jauntily.

A huge smile spread across Maisie's face as she picked him up and sat on the rug to cuddle him. 'I thought I'd never see you again!'

Flame rubbed the top of his soft little head against her chin. 'My uncle's spies have passed by. I am safe. For now.'

'Good! I hope those horrible mean things never come back!' Maisie said, through gritted teeth.

Flame looked up with serious green
eyes. 'They know I am close and they
will not stop looking for me. I may still
have to leave suddenly. Do you
understand that, Maisie?'

Maisie nodded, but she was
determined not to dwell on it. Her

wonderful magical friend was still here
and that was all she cared about. 'Let's
go downstairs. Mum bought some tins
of sardines the other day. Do you fancy
some?'

Flame gave an eager little mew.

'You look nice!' Maisie said to her
mum the following afternoon.

Mrs Simpson had pinned her hair up.
She wore sparkly earrings and a floaty
blue dress. 'Thanks, love,' she said, stretch-
ing cling film over a stack of sandwiches.

'What time are people coming?'
Maisie asked.

'In an hour or so I should imagine,'
her mum answered. 'The invitations said
after 4 p.m., but no one wants to be
the first to arrive. There, that's the food

finished. Would you take these through for me, please?'

Maisie nodded. Flame padded after her as she carefully carried the heaped plate into the gallery.

Flame seemed just like his old self. There was no trace of his nervousness of the day before. Maisie had convinced herself that his enemies had forgotten all about him and she smiled as she imagined the many adventures she and Flame would have together.

Mr Simpson was in the gallery setting out chairs. 'Well? What do you think?' he asked, as Maisie put the plate on a table already piled with delicious food.

Maisie looked round at the wooden floor and old counter, which now shone like dark honey. Paintings hung on the spotless white walls and colourful carved birds were on display in the modern cabinet.

'It's fantastic! Everyone's going to love it,' she said proudly.

Her dad came over to give her a hug. 'I think we're going to be very happy living here.'

'Definitely!' Maisie said, grinning. 'I wish Jane and Nina were already here, though. I hate waiting about when everything's ready.'

Her dad ruffled her hair. 'I think you've probably just got time to go down to the beach, if you're quick!'

Maisie flashed him a smile. She didn't need telling twice. 'Come on, Flame!'

As she zoomed out into the back garden, Flame gambolled along beside her. They had almost reached the garden gate when Maisie stopped suddenly.

Two powerful dark shapes were climbing up the steps from the beach. They gave a howl of rage as they smelt Flame. They hurled themselves against the closed gate with a crash!

Flame's enemies had found him!

'Save yourself, Flame!' she cried.

There was a bright flash. Where the tiny kitten had been now stood a magnificent young white lion and an older grey lion stood next to him.

'Prince Flame! We must leave now!' the grey lion growled urgently.

Flame turned to Maisie and his emerald eyes crinkled in a smile of farewell. 'Be well, be strong, Maisie,' he

said in a deep velvety growl as a rush
of sparks swirled round him. And then
he and the old lion were gone.

A harsh growl rang out as the dark
shapes burst through the gate and then
they too disappeared.

'Goodbye, Flame. I'll never forget
you,' Maisie said, her eyes filling with

tears. She was glad that Flame was safe. One day he would be king in his own world.

'Maisie! Oh, there you are. Jane and Nina are here! And Joel and Louise have just arrived!' called Mr Simpson from the back door.

Maisie wiped her eyes. She knew she was going to miss Flame dreadfully, but her spirits rose at the thought of seeing her old friends again. She had so much to talk to them about. As she turned and went into the house, she found herself smiling.

Win a Magic Kitten goody bag!

An urgent and secret message has been left for Flame
from his own world, where his evil uncle is
still hunting for him.

Two words from the message can be found in royal lion
crowns hidden in *Seaside Mystery* and *Firelight Friends*.
Find the hidden words and put them together to complete
the message. Send it in to us and each month we will
put every correct message in a draw and pick out one lucky
winner who will receive a purrfect Magic Kitten gift!

Send your secret message, name and address on a postcard to:
Magic Kitten Competition
Puffin Books
80 Strand
London WC2R 0RL

Hurry, Flame needs your help!

Good luck!

puffin.co.uk

Visit:
penguin.co.uk/static/cs/uk/0/competition/terms.html
for full terms and conditions

Magic Kitten

Firelight Friends

Flame needs to find a purrfect new friend!

And that's how Kara forgets all her troubles at summer camp when cute white kitten Flame turns up . . .

A cute kitten with little black paws needs a friend!

Magic Kitten

Firelight Friends

SUE BENTLEY

Magic Kitten

Classroom Chaos
978–0–141–32015–1

Double Trouble
978–0–141–32017–5

A Summer Spell
978–0–141–32014–4

Star Dreams
978–0–141–32016–8

Moonlight Mischief
978–0–141–32153–0

Sparkling Steps
978–0–141–32155–4

Firelight Friends
978-0-141-32199-8

A Circus Wish
978–0–141–32154–7

A Glittering Gallop
978–0–141–32156–1

Seaside Mystery
978–0–141–32198–1

puffin.co.uk